HOOWAY FOR WODNEY WAT

HELEN LESTER *Illustrated by* LYNN MUNSINGER

HOUGHTON MIFFLIN COMPANY BOSTON

Walter Lorraine Books

Walter Lorraine *wl* Books

Text copyright © 1999 by Helen Lester
Illustrations copyright © 1999 by Lynn Munsinger

www.houghtonmifflinbooks.com

Library of Congress Cataloging-in-Publication Data
Lester, Helen.
    Hooway for Wodney Wat / written by Helen Lester: illustrated by
Lynn Munsinger.
        p.   cm.
    Summary: All his classmates make fun of Rodney because he can't
pronounce his name, but it is Rodney's speech impediment that drives
away the class bully.
    CL ISBN 0-395-92392-1   PA ISBN 0-618-21612-X
    (1. Speech disorders—Fiction. 2. Schools—Fiction. 3. Bullies—Fiction.
4. Rodents—Fiction.) I. Munsinger, Lynn, ill. II. Title.
    PZ7.L56285Ho 1999
[E]—DC21   98-46149
                                                                     CIP
                                                                      AC

Printed in Mexico
WOZ 10 9 8

To my son — and hero — Jamie
HL

Poor Wodney.

Wodney Wat.

His real name was Rodney Rat, but he couldn't pronounce his *r*'s.

To make matters worse, he was a rodent. A wodent.

"What's your name, Wodney?" asked the other rodents.
"Wodney Wat," whispered Wodney.
"What's another name for bunny?" they asked knowingly.
"Wabbit," he mumbled.

"And how does a train travel?" They winked at each other.
"A twain twavels on twain twacks," Wodney replied miserably.

All of this teasing day in and
day out made Wodney the shyest
rodent in his elementary school.
His squeak could barely be heard in class.
He gnawed lunch alone.

And while the other rodents scurried and scooted about at recess, Wodney hid inside his jacket.

Then one day as the rodents were taking turns doing wheelies,
a new rodent — a very large rodent — barged into the classroom
and announced,
"My name is Camilla Capybara.

I'm bigger than any of you.
I'm meaner than any of you.
And I'm smarter than any of you."
Then she added, "So there."

With that she accidentally-on-purpose elbowed an ear, bumped two noses, stepped on three tails, and lay down on a desk.

Fur prickled in fear through the classroom.
She sure was bigger than any of them.
She sure looked meaner than any of them.
Was she smarter than any of them?

"What's 2 + 2?" asked Miss Fuzzleworth.

"FOUR!" shouted Camilla Capybara without even bothering to raise her paw. "And furthermore, 4 + 4 is 8, 8 + 8 is 16, and 243 +125 is 368."

Later, when Miss Fuzzleworth asked, "What's the capital of —"

Camilla interrupted, "New York. Albany. Population 295,594."
And during science, in answer to the question, "What part of a
plant is below the ground?" Camilla Capybara danced on her
desk and sang, "Root! Root! Rooty-toot-toot!"
"Yup," thought all the other rodents. "She's smarter than we are, too."
They felt very, very uncomfortable.

Every afternoon, just before the final recess, Miss Fuzzleworth
drew a name from her hat to see who would be the leader for their
favorite game, Simon Says. She scrunched her eyes closed and
jiggled the hat. Would it be Hairy Hamster? Minifeet Mouse?
Grizzlefriz Guinea Pig? Could it be big, mean, smart Camilla
Capybara?

Miss Fuzzleworth's paw reached in and pulled out the name of . . .
Wodney Wat!
The bell rang, there was a wild scurry for the door, and Camilla
Capybara was the first on the playground, having trampled the
others in her path.

To Wodney she looked
especially scary.

What would she do

when she heard him *speak*?

Breathe capybara breath in his face?

Or tie him up in his own tail?

Or even POUNCE on him?

The tiny, trembling leader of the game stood before the eager
players, his head well inside his jacket, and squeaked,

"Wodney says weed the sign."

While the other rodents read, "P.S. 142 ELEMENTARY SCHOOL FOR
RODENTS," Camilla began pulling up weeds around the sign and

wildly flinging them hither and yon till she was clear up to her
teeth in dirt.

The other rodents began to smile.

"Wodney says wap your paws awound your head."
He peeked a little peek out of his jacket and saw
WHAP! WHAP! WHAPPITY SLAPPITY WHAP! Camilla
was whapping her paws around her head so hard she
became dizzy, gave herself a headache, and had to sit down.
The other rodents couldn't help giggling.

"Wodney says play Wing Awound the Wosey."
Camilla put out her arms like wings and made an airplane noise.
"Nnnnrrrr."

But where was the wosey? WHAT was a wosey?

By now Wodney's voice was stronger and his head was entirely out of his jacket.

"Wake the leaves!"
Nobody moved.

"*Wodney says* wake the leaves!"

While Hairy, Minifeet, and Grizzlefriz and the others busied
themselves raking
Camilla Capybara grabbed one leaf.
"Wake up!" she yelled.

She snatched another. "Come on, you. Up, up, up!"

And another. "Rise and shine!"

And another. "BOO!"

By now all the other rodents were squealing with laughter.

All but Camilla, who frowned. "Stupid leaves. They won't wake up!"

And why was everyone laughing at her? Such bullies!

In a voice so strong he had to hold his own ears, Wodney called,
     "Wodney says go west!"
The rodents collapsed in a happy heap for a rest.
     Go west.

Camilla Capybara, feeling very smart that she could tell directions by the sun, said, "All right. I shall go west." And then she added, "So there."
West she stomped. Forever. She was gone.

And from that day on the pupils of P.S. 142 Elementary School for Rodents never teased Wodney again. He was their hero.
"Hooway for Wodney Wat!" they cried.
"Woot! Woot! Wooty-toot-toot!"